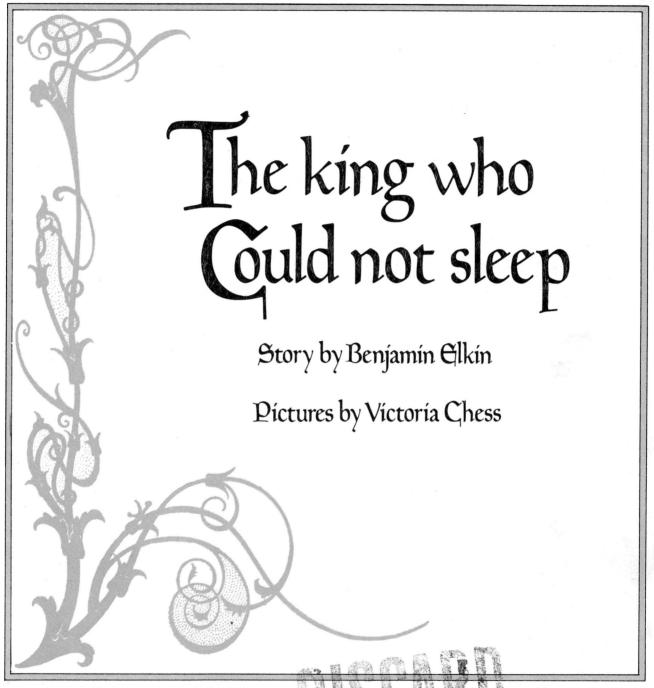

The king who Could not sleep

Story by Benjamin Elkin

Pictures by Victoria Chess

Parents' Magazine Press/New York

Text copyright © 1975 by Benjamin Elkin
Illustrations copyright © 1975 by Victoria Chess
Printed in the United States of America

Library of Congress Cataloging in Publication Data
Elkin, Benjamin.
   The king who could not sleep.
   SUMMARY: The Royal Council eliminates all noise from
the kingdom to help King Karl sleep, but to no avail.
   [1. Stories in rhyme] I. Chess, Victoria, illus.
II. Title.
PZ8.3.E44Ki   [E]   74-12444
ISBN 0-8193-0775-0
ISBN 0-8193-0776-9 (lib. bdg.)

To my sister, Rose Crimi,
with love and gratitude

Far beyond the ocean deep, on a mountain tall and steep,
there lived a king who COULD NOT SLEEP.
All night he tossed from side to side, but still
his eyes were open wide.

The Royal Council spoke its views. "We must help
poor King Karl to snooze.
Now what is it that quite destroys all blissful silence?
Why, it's NOISE.
The answer's plain, and we must try it: What King Karl
needs is *perfect quiet!*

"Remove those planes!" the Council said. "There's too much
roaring overhead.
And while you're at it, stop those trains . . . tear up the tracks
till none remains.
Move each hive of humming bees, and tie the whispering
leaves of trees."

Workmen labored night and day to move the airport far away.

Then they bent their aching backs to ripping up the railroad tracks.

They moved the hives of humming bees

and tied the whispering leaves of trees.

No roaring planes, no rushing trains,

no humming bees, no whispering trees.

But all this didn't help a mite. Poor King Karl was

UP ALL NIGHT.

"We've just begun," the Council said.

"We won't give up. Full speed ahead!"

So men put oil on squeaking doors, and thickest rugs
on creaking floors.

They blocked the kingdom's streets to cars, and took the crunch from candy bars.

No squeaking doors, no creaking floors,
   no honking cars, no crunching bars.
But King Karl tossed from side to side,

and still his eyes were OPEN WIDE.
"We will not stop," the Council stated,
"till ALL noise is eliminated."

They dammed the babbling of the brooks

and drove the birds from cozy nooks.

Clocks were not allowed to tick, nor locks to make
the slightest click.

Each subject walked about in socks, and children could not play with blocks.

No babbling brooks, no birds in nooks,

no ticking clocks, no clicking locks,

no shoes (just socks), no building blocks.

Yet every morn the dawn would break to find King Karl still
WIDE AWAKE!

The Council met in grave despair, glumly noting, "It isn't fair!
 One by one, see what we've done:
     No roaring planes,
     no rushing trains,
     no humming bees,
     no whispering trees,
     no squeaking doors,
     no creaking floors,
     no honking cars,

"no crunching bars,
no babbling brooks,
no birds in nooks,
no ticking clocks,
no clicking locks,
no shoes (just socks),
no building blocks.
What's left to do, for heaven's sake, to help King Karl be
UN-AWAKE?"

And as they wondered what was wrong, suddenly they heard a song.
The song was lovely, soft and low. But they had said
all noise must go! In anger, every Councilor rushed
to see what noise must now be hushed.

Up the stairs the Council hurried,
     down the halls the Council scurried.
Wan with worry, filled with gloom, in they ran to
     King Karl's room.

There, a new young nurse was sitting, sweetly crooning,
      calmly knitting. And her lovely lullabies
had closed—at last!—the young king's eyes.
Curled up snugly, breathing deep, baby Karl was
      FAST ASLEEP.